James Russell Lowell

My Garden Acquaintance and A Good Word for Winter

.

James Russell Lowell

My Garden Acquaintance and A Good Word for Winter

ISBN/EAN: 9783337083311

Printed in Europe, USA, Canada, Australia, Japan

Cover: Foto ©Andreas Hilbeck / pixelio.de

More available books at **www.hansebooks.com**

their contents makes them desirable always and everywhere. The series includes

STORIES, ESSAYS, SKETCHES, AND POEMS

SELECTED FROM THE WRITINGS OF

Emerson,	*Tennyson,*
Longfellow,	*Lowell,*
Whittier,	*Holmes,*
Hawthorne,	*Browning,*
Carlyle,	*Macaulay,*
Aldrich,	*Milton,*
Hood,	*Campbell,*
Gray,	*Owen Meredith,*
Aytoun,	*Pope,*

Thomson,

AND OTHERS OF EQUAL FAME.

The volumes are beautifully printed, many of them illustrated, and bound in flexible cloth covers, at a uniform price of

FIFTY CENTS EACH.

JAMES R. OSGOOD & CO.,
PUBLISHERS, BOSTON.

MY

GARDEN ACQUAINTANCE

and

A Good Word for Winter.

BY

JAMES RUSSELL LOWELL.

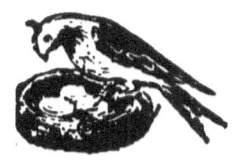

BOSTON:

JAMES R. OSGOOD AND COMPANY,

Late Ticknor and Fields, and Fields, Oogood, & Co.

1877.

University Press: Welch, Bigelow, & Co.,
Cambridge.

CONTENTS.

MY GARDEN ACQUAINTANCE.

NE of the most delightful books in my father's library was White's Natural History of Selborne. For me it has rather gained in charm with years. I used to read it without knowing the secret of the pleasure I found in it, but as I grow older I begin to detect some of the simple expedients of this natural magic. Open the book where you will, it takes you out of doors. In our broiling July weather one can walk out with this genially garrulous Fellow of Oriel and find refreshment instead of fatigue. You have no trouble in keeping abreast of him as he ambles along on his hobby-horse, now pointing to a pretty view, now stopping to watch the motions of a bird

or an insect, or to bag a specimen for the
Honorable Daines Barrington or Mr. Pen-
nant. In simplicity of taste and natural
refinement he reminds one of Walton ; in
tenderness toward what he would have called
the brute creation, of Cowper. I do not
know whether his descriptions of scenery are
good or not, but they have made me familiar
with his neighborhood. Since I first read
him, I have walked over some of his favorite haunts, but I still see them through his
eyes rather than by any recollection of actual
and personal vision. The book has also the
delightfulness of absolute leisure. Mr. White
seems never to have had any harder work to
do than to study the habits of his feathered
fellow-townsfolk, or to watch the ripening
of his peaches on the wall. His volumes
are the journal of Adam in Paradise,

> " Annihilating all that 's made
> To a green thought in a green shade."

It is positive rest only to look into that garden of his. It is vastly better than to

> " See great Diocletian walk
> In the Salonian garden's noble shade,"

for thither ambassadors intrude to bring with them the noises of Rome, while here the world has no entrance. No rumor of the revolt of the American Colonies seems to have reached him. " The natural term of an hog's life" has more interest for him than that of an empire. Burgoyne may surrender and welcome ; of what consequence is *that* compared with the fact that we can explain the odd tumbling of rooks in the air by their turning over "to scratch themselves with one claw" ? All the couriers in Europe spurring rowel-deep make no stir in Mr. White's little Chartreuse ; but the arrival of the house-martin a day earlier or later than last year is a piece of news worth sending express to all his correspondents.

Another secret charm of this book is its inadvertent humor, so much the more delicious because unsuspected by the author. How pleasant is his innocent vanity in adding to the list of the British, and still more of the Selbornian, *fauna !* I believe he would gladly have consented to be eaten by a tiger or a crocodile, if by that means the occasional

presence within the parish limits of either
of these anthropophagous brutes could have
been established. He brags of no fine society, but is plainly a little elated by "having considerable acquaintance with a tame
brown owl." Most of us have known our
share of owls, but few can boast of intimacy
with a feathered one. The great events of
Mr. White's life, too, have that dispropor-
tionate importance which is always humor-
ous. To think of his hands having actually
been thought worthy (as neither Willough-
by's nor Ray's were) to hold a stilted plover,
the *Charadrius himantopus*, with no back toe,
and therefore "liable, in speculation, to perpetual vacillations"! I wonder, by the way,
if metaphysicians have no hind toes. In
1770 he makes the acquaintance in Sussex
of "an old family tortoise," which had then
been domesticated for thirty years. It is
clear that he fell in love with it at first
sight. We have no means of tracing the
growth of his passion; but in 1780 we find
him eloping with its object in a post-chaise.
"The rattle and hurry of the journey so per-

fectly roused it that, when I turned it out in a border, it walked twice down to the bottom of my garden." It reads like a Court Journal : "Yesterday morning H. R. H. the Princess Alice took an airing of half an hour on the terrace of Windsor Castle." This tortoise might have been a member of the Royal Society, if he could have condescended to so ignoble an ambition. It had but just been discovered that a surface inclined at a certain angle with the plane of the horizon took more of the sun's rays. The tortoise had always known this (though he unostentatiously made no parade of it), and used accordingly to tilt himself up against the garden-wall in the autumn. He seems to have been more of a philosopher than even Mr. White himself, caring for nothing but to get under a cabbage-leaf when it rained, or the sun was too hot, and to bury himself alive before frost, — a four-footed Diogenes, who carried his tub on his back.

There are moods in which this kind of history is infinitely refreshing. These creatures whom we affect to look down upon as

the drudges of instinct are members of a
commonwealth whose constitution rests on
immovable bases. Never any need of re-
construction there! *They* never dream of
settling it by vote that eight hours are equal
to ten, or that one creature is as clever as
another and no more. *They* do not use their
poor wits in regulating God's clocks, nor
think they cannot go astray so long as they
carry their guide-board about with them, —
a delusion we often practise upon ourselves
with our high and mighty reason, that admirable finger-post which points every way
and always right. It is good for us now
and then to converse with a world like Mr.
White's, where Man is the least important
of animals. But one who, like me, has always lived in the country and always on the
same spot, is drawn to his book by other
occult sympathies. Do we not share his
indignation at that stupid Martin who had
graduated his thermometer no lower than 4°
above zero of Fahrenheit, so that in the cold-
est weather ever known the mercury basely
absconded into the bulb, and left us to see

the victory slip through our fingers just as
they were closing upon it ? No man, I suspect, ever lived long in the country without
being bitten by these meteorological ambi-
tions.   He likes to be hotter and colder, to
have been more deeply snowed up, to have
more trees and larger blown down than his
neighbors.   With us descendants of the Pu-
ritans especially, these weather-competitions
supply the abnegated excitement of the race-
course.   Men learn to value thermometers
of the true imaginative temperament, capable of prodigious elations and correspond-
ing dejections.   The other day (5th July) I
marked 98° in the shade, my high-water
mark, higher by one degree than I had ever
seen it before.   I happened to meet a neighbor ; as we mopped our brows at each other,
he told me that he had just cleared 100°,
and I went home a beaten man.   I had not
felt the heat before, save as a beautiful exag-
geration of sunshine ; but now it oppressed
me with the prosaic vulgarity of an oven.
What had been poetic intensity became all
at once rhetorical hyperbole.   I might sus-

pect his thermometer (as indeed I did, for
we Harvard men are apt to think ill of any
graduation but our own) ; but it was a poor
consolation. The fact remained that his her-
ald Mercury, standing a-tiptoe, could look
down on mine. I seem to glimpse something of this familiar weakness in Mr. White.
He, too, has shared in these mercurial tri-
umphs and defeats. Nor do I doubt that
he had a true country-gentleman's interest
in the weathercock ; that his first question
on coming down of a morning was, like
Barabbas's,

"Into what quarter peers my halcyon's bill ?"

It is an innocent and healthful employment of the mind, distracting one from too
continual study of himself, and leading him
to dwell rather upon the indigestions of the
elements than his own. "Did the wind
back round, or go about with the sun ?" is
a rational question that bears not remotely
on the making of hay and the prosperity of
crops. I have little doubt that the regulated
observation of the vane in many different

places, and the interchange of results by tel-
egraph, would put the weather, as it were,
in our power, by betraying its ambushes before it is ready to give the assault. At first
sight, nothing seems more drolly trivial than
the lives of those whose single achievement
is to record the wind and the temperature
three times a day. Yet such men are doubtless sent into the world for this special end,
and perhaps there is no kind of accurate observation, whatever its object, that has not
its final use and value for some one or other.
It is even to be hoped that the speculations
of our newspaper editors and their myriad
correspondents upon the signs of the political
atmosphere may also fill their appointed place
in a well-regulated universe, if it be only
that of supplying so many more jack-o'-lan-
terns to the future historian. Nay, the ob-
servations on finance of an M. C. whose sole
knowledge of the subject has been derived
from a lifelong success in getting a living
out of the public without paying any equiv-
alent therefor, will perhaps be of interest
hereafter to some explorer of our *cloaca
maxima*, whenever it is cleansed.

For many years I have been in the habit
of noting down some of the leading events
of my embowered solitude, such as the coming of certain birds and the like, — a kind
of *mémoires pour servir*, after the fashion of
White, rather than properly digested natural
history.   I thought it not impossible that a
few simple stories of my winged acquaint-
ances might be found entertaining by per-
sons of kindred taste.

There is a common notion that animals
are better meteorologists than men, and I
have little doubt that in immediate weather-
wisdom they have the advantage of our so-
phisticated senses (though I suspect a sailor
or shepherd would be their match), but I
have seen nothing that leads me to believe
their minds capable of erecting the horoscope
of a whole season, and letting us know be-
forehand whether the winter will be severe
or the summer rainless.   I more than suspect that the clerk of the weather himself
does not always know very long in advance
whether he is to draw an order for hot or
cold, dry or moist, and the musquash is

scarce likely to be wiser. I have noted but two days' difference in the coming of the song-sparrow between a very early and a very backward spring. This very year I saw the linnets at work thatching, just before a snow-storm which covered the ground several inches deep for a number of days. They struck work and left us for a while, no doubt in search of food. Birds frequently perish from sudden changes in our whimsical spring weather of which they had no foreboding. More than thirty years ago, a cherry-tree, then in full bloom, near my window, was covered with humming-birds benumbed by a fall of mingled rain and snow, which probably killed many of them. It should seem that their coming was dated by the height of the sun, which betrays them into unthrifty matrimony ;

"So nature pricketh hem in their corages";

but their going is another matter. The chimney-swallows leave us early, for example, apparently so soon as their latest fledglings are firm enough of wing to attempt the

long rowing-match that is before them. On
the other hand, the wild-geese probably do
not leave the North till they are frozen out,
for I have heard their bugles sounding south-
ward so late as the middle of December.
What may be called local migrations are
doubtless dictated by the chances of food.
I have once been visited by large flights
of cross-bills ; and whenever the snow lies
long and deep on the ground, a flock of
cedar-birds comes in midwinter to eat the
berries on my hawthorns.   I have never
been quite able to fathom the local, or rather
geographical partialities of birds.   Never before this summer (1870) have the king-birds,
handsomest of fly-catchers, built in my orchard ; though I always know where to find
them within half a mile.   The rose-breasted
grosbeak has been a familiar bird in Brook-
line (three miles away), yet I never saw one
here till last July, when I found a female
busy among my raspberries and surprisingly
bold.   I hope she was *prospecting* with a view
to settlement in our garden.   She seemed,
on the whole, to think well of my fruit, and

I would gladly plant another bed if it would help to win over so delightful a neighbor.

The return of the robin is commonly announced by the newspapers, like that of eminent or notorious people to a watering-place, as the first authentic notification of spring. And such his appearance in the orchard and garden undoubtedly is. But, in spite of his name of migratory thrush, he stays with us all winter, and I have seen him when the thermometer marked 15° below zero of Fahrenheit, armed impregnably within, like Emerson's Titmouse, and as cheerful as he. The robin has a bad reputation among people who do not value themselves less for being fond of cherries. There is, I admit, a spice of vulgarity in him, and his song is rather of the Bloomfield sort, too largely ballasted with prose. His ethics are of the Poor Richard school, and the main chance which calls forth all his energy is altogether of the belly. He never has those fine intervals of lunacy into which his cousins, the catbird and the mavis, are apt to fall. But for a' that and twice as muckle 's a' that, I would not exchange him for all the cherries that ever came out of Asia Minor. With whatever faults, he has not wholly forfeited that superiority which belongs to the children of nature. He has a finer taste in fruit than could be distilled from many successive committees of the Horticultural Society, and he eats with a relishing gulp not inferior to Dr. Johnson's. He feels and freely exercises his right of eminent domain. His is the earliest mess of green peas ; his all the mulberries I had fancied mine. But if he get also the lion's share of the raspberries, he is a great planter, and sows those wild ones in the woods, that solace the pedestrian and give a momentary calm even to the jaded victims of the White Hills. He keeps a strict eye over one's fruit, and knows to a shade of purple when your grapes have cooked long enough in the sun. During the severe drought a few years ago, the robins wholly vanished from my garden. I neither saw nor heard one for three weeks. Meanwhile a small foreign grape-vine, rather shy of bearing, seemed to find the dusty air congenial, and, dreaming perhaps of its sweet Argos across the sea, decked itself with a score or so of fair bunches. I watched them from day to day till they should have secreted sugar enough from the sunbeams, and at last made up my mind that I would celebrate my vintage the next morning. But the robins too had somehow kept note of them. They must have sent out spies, as did the Jews into the promised land, before I was stirring. When I went with my basket, at least a dozen of these winged vintagers bustled out from among the leaves, and alighting on the nearest trees interchanged some shrill remarks about me of a derogatory nature. They had fairly sacked the vine. Not Wellington's veterans made cleaner work of a Spanish town ; not Federals or Confederates were ever more impartial in the confiscation of neutral chickens. I was keeping my grapes a secret to surprise the fair Fidele with, but the robins made them a profounder secret to her than I had meant. The tattered remnant of a single bunch was all my harvest-home. How paltry it looked at the bottom of my basket, — as if a humming-bird had laid her egg in an eagle's nest ! I could not help laughing ; and the robins seemed to join heartily in the merriment. There was a native grape-vine close by, blue with its less refined abundance, but my cunning thieves preferred the foreign flavor. Could I tax them with want of taste ?

The robins are not good solo singers, but their chorus, as, like primitive fire-worshippers, they hail the return of light and warmth to the world, is unrivalled. There are a hundred singing like one. They are noisy enough then, and sing, as poets should, with no afterthought. But when they come after cherries to the tree near my window, they muffle their voices, and their faint *pip, pip, pop !* sounds far away at the bottom of the garden, where they know I shall not suspect them of robbing the great black-walnut of its bitter-rinded store.* They are feathered

---

* The screech-owl, whose cry, despite his ill name, is one of the sweetest sounds in nature, softens his voice in the same way with the most beguiling mockery of distance.

Pecksniffs, to be sure, but then how brightly their breasts, that look rather shabby in the sunlight, shine in a rainy day against the dark green of the fringe-tree! After they have pinched and shaken all the life out of an earthworm, as Italian cooks pound all the spirit out of a steak, and then gulped him, they stand up in honest self-confidence, expand their red waistcoats with the virtuous air of a lobby member, and outface you with an eye that calmly challenges inquiry. "Do *I* look like a bird that knows the flavor of raw vermin? I throw myself upon a jury of my peers. Ask any robin if he ever ate anything less ascetic than the frugal berry of the juniper, and he will answer that his vow forbids him." Can such an open bosom cover such depravity? Alas, yes! I have no doubt his breast was redder at that very moment with the blood of my raspberries. On the whole, he is a doubtful friend in the garden. He makes his dessert of all kinds of berries, and is not averse from early pears. But when we remember how omnivorous he is, eating his own weight in an incredibly short time, and that Nature seems exhaustless in her invention of new insects hostile to vegetation, perhaps we may reckon that he does more good than harm. For my own part, I would rather have his cheerfulness and kind neighborhood than many berries.

For his cousin, the catbird, I have a still warmer regard. Always a good singer, he sometimes nearly equals the brown thrush, and has the merit of keeping up his music later in the evening than any bird of my familiar acquaintance. Ever since I can remember, a pair of them have built in a gigantic syringa, near our front door, and I have known the male to sing almost uninterruptedly during the evenings of early summer till twilight duskened into dark. They differ greatly in vocal talent, but all have a delightful way of crooning over, and, as it were, rehearsing their song in an undertone, which makes their nearness always unobtrusive. Though there is the most trustworthy witness to the imitative propensity of this bird, I have only once, during an intimacy of more than forty years, heard him indulge it.   In that case, the imitation was by no means so close as to deceive, but a free reproduction of the notes of some other birds, especially of the oriole, as a kind of variation in his own song.   The catbird is as shy as the robin is vulgarly familiar.   Only when his nest or his fledglings are approached does he become noisy and almost aggressive. I have known him to station his young in a thick cornel-bush on the edge of the rasp-berry-bed, after the fruit began to ripen, and feed them there for a week or more.   In such cases he shows none of that conscious guilt which makes the robin contemptible.   On the contrary, he will maintain his post in the thicket, and sharply scold the intruder who ventures to steal *his* berries.   After all, his claim is only for tithes, while the robin will bag your entire crop if he get a chance.

Dr. Watts's statement that "birds in their little nests agree," like too many others in-tended to form the infant mind, is very far from being true.   On the contrary, the most peaceful relation of the different species to each other is that of armed neutrality.   They are very jealous of neighbors. A few years ago, I was much interested in the house-building of a pair of summer yellow-birds. They had chosen a very pretty site near the top of a tall white lilac, within easy eye-shot of a chamber window. A very pleasant thing it was to see their little home growing with mutual help, to watch their industrious skill interrupted only by little flirts and snatches of endearment, frugally cut short by the common-sense of the tiny housewife. They had brought their work nearly to an end, and had already begun to line it with fern-down, the gathering of which demanded more distant journeys and longer absences. But, alas! the syringa, immemorial manor of the catbirds, was not more than twenty feet away, and these "giddy neighbors" had, as it appeared, been all along jealously watch-ful, though silent, witnesses of what they deemed an intrusion of squatters. No sooner were the pretty mates fairly gone for a new load of lining, than

> "To their unguarded nest these weasel Scots
> Came stealing."

Silently they flew back and forth, each giving a vengeful dab at the nest in passing. They did not fall-to and deliberately destroy it, for they might have been caught at their mischief. As it was, whenever the yellow-birds came back, their enemies were hidden in their own sight-proof bush. Several times their unconscious victims repaired damages, but at length, after counsel taken together, they gave it up. Perhaps, like other unlettered folk, they came to the conclusion that the Devil was in it, and yielded to the invisible persecutions of witchcraft.

The robins, by constant attacks and annoyances, have succeeded in driving off the blue-jays who used to build in our pines, their gay colors and quaint noisy ways making them welcome and amusing neighbors. I once had the chance of doing a kindness to a household of them, which they received with very friendly condescension. I had had my eye for some time upon a nest, and was puzzled by a constant fluttering of what seemed full-grown wings in it whenever I drew nigh. At last I climbed the tree, in

spite of angry protests from the old birds
against my intrusion. The mystery had a
very simple solution. In building the nest,
a long piece of packthread had been somewhat loosely woven in. Three of the young
had contrived to entangle themselves in it,
and had become full-grown without being
able to launch themselves upon the air.
One was unharmed ; another had so tightly
twisted the cord about its shank that one
foot was curled up and seemed paralyzed ;
the third, in its struggles to escape, had
sawn through the flesh of the thigh and so
much harmed itself that I thought it hu-
mane to put an end to its misery. When I
took out my knife to cut their hempen bonds,
the heads of the family seemed to divine
my friendly intent. Suddenly ceasing their
cries and threats, they perched quietly within reach of my hand, and watched me in my
work of manumission. This, owing to the
fluttering terror of the prisoners, was an
affair of some delicacy ; but erelong I was
rewarded by seeing one of them fly away to
a neighboring tree, while the cripple, making

a parachute of his wings, came lightly to the ground, and hopped off as well as he could with one leg, obsequiously waited on by his elders. A week later I had the satisfaction of meeting him in the pine-walk, in good spirits, and already so far recovered as to be able to balance himself with the lame foot. I have no doubt that in his old age he accounted for his lameness by some handsome story of a wound received at the famous Battle of the Pines, when our tribe, overcome by numbers, was driven from its ancient camping-ground. Of late years the jays have visited us only at intervals; and in winter their bright plumage, set off by the snow, and their cheerful cry, are especially welcome. They would have furnished Æsop with a fable, for the feathered crest in which they seem to take so much satisfaction is often their fatal snare. Country boys make a hole with their finger in the snow-crust just large enough to admit the jay's head, and, hollowing it out somewhat beneath, bait it with a few kernels of corn. The crest slips easily into the trap, but refuses to be pulled out again, and he who came to feast remains a prey.

Twice have the crow-blackbirds attempted a settlement in my pines, and twice have the robins, who claim a right of pre-emption, so successfully played the part of border-ruffians as to drive them away, — to my great regret, for they are the best substitute we have for rooks. At Shady Hill (now, alas ! empty of its so long-loved household) they build by hundreds, and nothing can be more cheery than their creaking clatter (like a convention of old-fashioned tavern-signs) as they gather at evening to debate in mass meeting their windy politics, or to gossip at their tent-doors over the events of the day. Their port is grave, and their stalk across the turf as martial as that of a second-rate ghost in Hamlet. They never meddled with my corn, so far as I could discover.

For a few years I had crows, but their nests are an irresistible bait for boys, and their settlement was broken up. They grew so wonted as to throw off a great part of their shyness, and to tolerate my near approach. One very hot day I stood for some time within twenty feet of a mother and three children, who sat on an elm bough over my head, gasping in the sultry air, and holding their wings half-spread for coolness. All birds during the pairing season become more or less sentimental, and murmur soft nothings in a tone very unlike the grinding-organ repetition and loudness of their habitual song. The crow is very comical as a lover, and to hear him trying to soften his croak to the proper Saint Preux standard, has something the effect of a Mississippi boatman quoting Tennyson. Yet there are few things to my ear more melodious than his caw of a clear winter morning as it drops to you filtered through five hundred fathoms of crisp blue air. The hostility of all smaller birds makes the moral character of the crow, for all his deaconlike demeanor and garb, somewhat questionable. He could never sally forth without insult. The golden robins, especially, would chase him as far as I could follow with my eye, making him duck clumsily to avoid their importunate bills. I

do not believe, however, that he robbed any
nests hereabouts, for the refuse of the gas-
works, which, in our free-and-easy commu-
nity, is allowed to poison the river, supplied
him with dead alewives in abundance. I
used to watch him making his periodical
visits to the salt-marshes and coming back
with a fish in his beak to his young savages,
who, no doubt, like it in that condition
which makes it savory to the Kanakas and
other corvine races of men.

Orioles are in great plenty with me. I
have seen seven males flashing about the
garden at once. A merry crew of them
swing their hammocks from the pendulous
boughs. During one of these latter years,
when the canker-worms stripped our elms
as bare as winter, these birds went to the
trouble of rebuilding their unroofed nests,
and chose for the purpose trees which are
safe from those swarming vandals, such as
the ash and the button-wood. One year a
pair (disturbed, I suppose, elsewhere) built
a second nest in an elm, within a few yards
of the house. My friend, Edward E. Hale,

told me once that the oriole rejected from
his web all strands of brilliant color, and I
thought it a striking example of that instinct of concealment noticeable in many
birds, though it should seem in this instance
that the nest was amply protected by its
position from all marauders but owls and
squirrels.   Last year, however, I had the
fullest proof that Mr. Hale was mistaken.
A pair of orioles built on the lowest trailer
of a weeping elm, which hung within ten
feet of our drawing-room window, and so
low that I could reach it from the ground.
The nest was wholly woven and felted with
ravellings of woollen carpet in which scarlet
predominated.   Would the same thing have
happened in the woods?   Or did the nearness of a human dwelling perhaps give the
birds a greater feeling of security?   They
are very bold, by the way, in quest of cord-
age, and I have often watched them strip-
ping the fibrous bark from a honeysuckle
growing over the very door.   But, indeed,
all my birds look upon me as if I were a
mere tenant at will, and they were land-

lords. With shame I confess it, I have been
bullied even by a humming-bird. This
spring, as I was cleansing a pear-tree of its
lichens, one of these little zigzagging blurs
came purring toward me, couching his long
bill like a lance, his throat sparkling with
angry fire, to warn me off from a Missouri-
currant whose honey he was sipping. And
many a time he has driven me out of a
flower-bed. This summer, by the way, a
pair of these winged emeralds fastened their
mossy acorn-cup upon a bough of the same
elm which the orioles had enlivened the
year before. We watched all their proceed-
ings from the window through an opera-
glass, and saw their two nestlings grow from
black needles with a tuft of down at the
lower end, till they whirled away on their
first short experimental flights. They became strong of wing in a surprisingly short
time, and I never saw them or the male bird
after, though the female was regular as usual
in her visits to our petunias and verbenas.
I do not think it ground enough for a gen-
eralization, but in the many times when I

watched the old birds feeding their young, the mother always alighted, while the father as uniformly remained upon the wing.

The bobolinks are generally chance visitors, tinkling through the garden in blossoming-time, but this year, owing to the long rains early in the season, their favorite meadows were flooded, and they were driven to the upland. So I had a pair of them domiciled in my grass-field. The male used to perch in an apple-tree, then in full bloom, and, while I stood perfectly still close by, he would circle away, quivering round the entire field of five acres, with no break in his song, and settle down again among the blossoms, to be hurried away almost immediately by a new rapture of music. He had the volubility of an Italian charlatan at a fair, and, like him, appeared to be proclaiming the merits of some quack remedy. *Opodeldoc-opodeldoc-try-Doctor-Lincoln's-opodeldoc !* he seemed to repeat over and over again, with a rapidity that would have distanced the deftest-tongued Figaro that ever rattled. I remember Count Gurowski saying once,

with that easy superiority of knowledge
about this country which is the monopoly
of foreigners, that we had no singing-birds!
Well, well, Mr. Hepworth Dixon has found
the typical America in Oneida and Salt
Lake City. Of course, an intelligent Euro-
pean is the best judge of these matters.
The truth is there are more singing-birds
in Europe because there are fewer forests.
These songsters love the neighborhood of
man because hawks and owls are rarer,
while their own food is more abundant.
Most people seem to think, the more trees,
the more birds. Even Châteaubriand, who
first tried the primitive-forest-cure, and
whose description of the wilderness in its
imaginative effects is unmatched, fancies the
"people of the air singing their hymns to
him." So far as my own observation goes,
the farther one penetrates the sombre soli-
tudes of the woods, the more seldom does
he hear the voice of any singing-bird. In
spite of Châteaubriand's minuteness of de-
tail, in spite of that marvellous reverberation of the decrepit tree falling of its own

weight, which he was the first to notice, I cannot help doubting whether he made his way very deep into the wilderness. At any rate, in a letter to Fontanes, written in 1804, he speaks of *mes chevaux paissant à quelque distance.* To be sure Châteaubriand was apt to mount the high horse, and this may have been but an afterthought of the *grand seigneur,* but certainly one would not make much headway on horseback toward the druid fastnesses of the primeval pine.

The bobolinks build in considerable numbers in a meadow within a quarter of a mile of us. A houseless lane passes through the midst of their camp, and in clear westerly weather, at the right season, one may hear a score of them singing at once. When they are breeding, if I chance to pass, one of the male birds always accompanies me like a constable, flitting from post to post of the rail-fence, with a short note of reproof continually repeated, till I am fairly out of the neighborhood. Then he will swing away into the air and run down the wind, gurgling music without stint over the unheeding tussocks of meadow-grass and dark clumps of bulrushes that mark his domain.

We have no bird whose song will match the nightingale's in compass, none whose note is so rich as that of the European blackbird ; but for mere rapture I have never heard the bobolink's rival. But his opera-season is a short one. The ground and tree sparrows are our most constant performers. It is now late in August, and one of the latter sings every day and all day long in the garden. Till within a fortnight, a pair of indigo-birds would keep up their lively *duo* for an hour together. While I write, I hear an oriole gay as in June, and the plaintive *may-be* of the goldfinch tells me he is stealing my lettuce-seeds. I know not what the experience of others may have been, but the only bird I have ever heard sing in the night has been the chip-bird. I should say he sang about as often during the darkness as cocks crow. One can hardly help fancying that he sings in his dreams.

"Father of light, what sunnie seed,
 What glance of day hast thou confined

Into this bird?   To all the breed
This busie ray thou hast assigned ;
Their magnetism works all night,
And dreams of Paradise and light."

On second thought, I remember to have heard the cuckoo strike the hours nearly all night with the regularity of a Swiss clock.

The dead limbs of our elms, which I spare to that end, bring us the flicker every summer, and almost daily I hear his wild scream and laugh close at hand, himself invisible. He is a shy bird, but a few days ago I had the satisfaction of studying him through the blinds as he sat on a tree within a few feet of me.   Seen so near and at rest, he makes good his claim to the title of pigeon-wood-pecker.   Lumberers have a notion that he is harmful to timber, digging little holes through the bark to encourage the settlement of insects.   The regular rings of such perforations which one may see in almost any apple-orchard seem to give some probability to this theory.   Almost every season a solitary quail visits us, and, unseen among the currant-bushes, calls *Bob White, Bob*

White, as if he were playing at hide-and-seek with that imaginary being. A rarer visitant is the turtle-dove, whose pleasant coo (something like the muffled crow of a cock from a coop covered with snow) I have sometimes heard, and whom I once had the good luck to see close by me in the mulberry-tree. The wild-pigeon, once numerous, I have not seen for many years.* Of savage birds, a hen-hawk now and then quarters himself upon us for a few days, sitting sluggish in a tree after a surfeit of poultry. One of them once offered me a near shot from my study-window one drizzly day for several hours. But it was Sunday, and I gave him the benefit of its gracious truce of God.

Certain birds have disappeared from our neighborhood within my memory. I remember when the whippoorwill could be heard in Sweet Auburn. The night-hawk, once common, is now rare. The brown thrush has moved farther up country. For

* They made their appearance again this summer (1870).

years I have not seen or heard any of the larger owls, whose hooting was one of my boyish terrors.   The cliff-swallow, strange emigrant, that eastward takes his way, has come and gone again in my time.   The bank-swallows, wellnigh innumerable during my boyhood, no longer frequent the crumbly cliff of the gravel-pit by the river.   The barn-swallows, which once swarmed in our barn, flashing through the dusty sun-streaks of the mow, have been gone these many years.   My father would lead me out to see them gather on the roof, and take counsel before their yearly migration, as Mr. White used to see them at Selborne.   *Eheu, fugaces!* Thank fortune, the swift still glues his nest, and rolls his distant thunders night and day in the wide-throated chimneys, still sprinkles the evening air with his merry twittering. The populous heronry in Fresh Pond meadows has been wellnigh broken up, but still a pair or two haunt the old home, as the gypsies of Ellangowan their ruined huts, and every evening fly over us riverwards, clearing their throats with a hoarse hawk

as they go, and, in cloudy weather, scarce
higher than the tops of the chimneys. Sometimes I have known one to alight in one of
our trees, though for what purpose I never
could divine. Kingfishers have sometimes
puzzled me in the same way, perched at
high noon in a pine, springing their watchman's rattle when they flitted away from my
curiosity, and seeming to shove their top-
heavy heads along as a man does a wheel-
barrow.

Some birds have left us, I suppose, because
the country is growing less wild. I once
found a summer duck's nest within quarter
of a mile of our house, but such a *trouvaille*
would be impossible now as Kidd's treasure.
And yet the mere taming of the neighborhood does not quite satisfy me as an expla-
nation. Twenty years ago, on my way to
bathe in the river, I saw every day a brace
of woodcock, on the miry edge of a spring
within a few rods of a house, and constantly
visited by thirsty cows. There was no growth
of any kind to conceal them, and yet these
ordinarily shy birds were almost as indiffer-

ent to my passing as common poultry would
have been.   Since bird-nesting has become
scientific, and dignified itself as oölogy, that,
no doubt, is partly to blame for some of our
losses.   But some old friends are constant.
Wilson's thrush comes every year to remind
me of that most poetic of ornithologists.   He
flits before me through the pine-walk like
the very genius of solitude.   A pair of pewees have built immemorially on a jutting
brick in the arched entrance to the ice-house.
Always on the same brick, and never more
than a single pair, though two broods of five
each are raised there every summer.   How
do they settle their claim to the homestead ?
By what right of primogeniture ?   Once the
children of a man employed about the place
oölogized the nest, and the pewees left us for
a year or two.   I felt towards those boys as
the messmates of the Ancient Mariner did
towards him after he had shot the albatross.
But the pewees came back at last, and one
of them is now on his wonted perch, so near
my window that I can hear the click of his
bill as he snaps a fly on the wing with

the unerring precision a stately Trasteverina shows in the capture of her smaller deer. The pewee is the first bird to pipe up in the morning ; and during the early summer he preludes his matutinal ejaculation of *pewee* with a slender whistle, unheard at any other time. He saddens with the season, and, as summer declines, he changes his note to *eheu, pewee !* as if in lamentation. Had he been an Italian bird, Ovid would have had a plaintive tale to tell about him. He is so familiar as often to pursue a fly through the open window into my library.

There is something inexpressibly dear to me in these old friendships of a lifetime. There is scarce a tree of mine but has had, at some time or other, a happy homestead among its boughs, to which I cannot say,

> " Many light hearts and wings,
> Which now be dead, lodged in thy living bowers."

My walk under the pines would lose half its summer charm were I to miss that shy anchorite, the Wilson's thrush, nor hear in haying-time the metallic ring of his song, that justifies his rustic name of *scythe-whet*. I protect my game as jealously as an English squire. If anybody had oölogized a certain cuckoo's nest I know of (I have a pair in my garden every year), it would have left me a sore place in my mind for weeks. I love to bring these aborigines back to the mansuetude they showed to the early voyagers, and before (forgive the involuntary pun) they had grown accustomed to man and knew his savage ways. And they repay your kindness with a sweet familiarity too delicate ever to breed contempt. I have made a Penn-treaty with them, preferring that to the Puritan way with the natives, which converted them to a little Hebraism and a great deal of Medford rum. If they will not come near enough to me (as most of them will), I bring them close with an opera-glass, — a much better weapon than a gun. I would not, if I could, convert them from their pretty pagan ways. The only one I sometimes have savage doubts about is the red squirrel. I *think* he oölogizes. I *know* he eats cherries (we counted five of them at one time in a single tree, the stones pattering down like the sparse hail that preludes a storm), and that he gnaws off the small end of pears to get at the seeds. He steals the corn from under the noses of my poultry. But what would you have? He will come down upon the limb of the tree I am lying under till he is within a yard of me. He and his mate will scurry up and down the great black-walnut for my diversion, chattering like monkeys. Can I sign his death-warrant who has tolerated me about his grounds so long? Not I. Let them steal, and welcome. I am sure I should, had I had the same bringing up and the same temptation. As for the birds, I do not believe there is one of them but does more good than harm ; and of how many featherless bipeds can this be said?

A GOOD WORD FOR WINTER.

EN scarcely know how beautiful fire is," says Shelley ; and I am apt to think there are a good many other things concerning which their knowledge might be largely increased without becoming burdensome. Nor are they altogether reluctant to be taught, — not so reluctant, perhaps, as unable, — and education is sure to find one fulcrum ready to her hand by which to get a purchase on them. For most of us, I have noticed, are not without an amiable willingness to assist at any spectacle or entertainment (loosely so called) for which no fee is charged at the door. If special tickets are sent us, another element of pleasure is added in a sense of privilege and pre-

eminence (pitiably scarce in a democracy) so
deeply rooted in human nature that I have
seen people take a strange satisfaction in
being near of kin to the mute chief person-
age in a funeral. It gave them a moment's
advantage over the rest of us whose grief
was rated at a lower place in the procession.
But the words "admission free" at the
bottom of a handbill, though holding out no
bait of inequality, have yet a singular charm
for many minds, especially in the country.
There is something touching in the con-
stancy with which men attend free lectures,
and in the honest patience with which they
listen to them. He who pays may yawn or
shift testily in his seat, or even go out with
an awful reverberation of criticism, for he has
bought the right to do any or all of these
and paid for it. But gratuitous hearers are
anæsthetized to suffering by a sense of virtue.
They are performing perhaps the noblest,
as it is one of the most difficult, of human
functions in getting Something (no matter
how small) for Nothing. They are not pes-
tered by the awful duty of securing their

money's worth.   They are wasting time, to
do which elegantly and without lassitude is
the highest achievement of civilization.   If
they are cheated, it is, at worst, only of a
superfluous hour which was rotting on their
hands.   Not only is mere amusement made
more piquant, but instruction more palata-
ble, by this universally relished sauce of
gratuity.   And if the philosophic observer
finds an object of agreeable contemplation
in the audience, as they listen to a discourse
on the probability of making missionaries
go down better with the Feejee-Islanders by
balancing the hymn-book in one pocket
with a bottle of Worcestershire in the other,
or to a plea for arming the female gorilla
with the ballot, he also takes a friendly interest in the lecturer, and admires the wise
economy of Nature who thus contrives an
ample field of honest labor for her bores.
Even when the insidious hat is passed round
after one of these eleemosynary feasts, the
relish is but heightened by a conscientious
refusal to disturb the satisfaction's complete-
ness with the rattle of a single contributory

penny. So firmly persuaded am I of this
gratis-instinct in our common humanity,
that I believe I could fill a house by adver-
tising a free lecture on Tupper considered as
a philosophic poet, or on my personal recol-
lections of the late James K. Polk. This
being so, I have sometimes wondered that
the peep-shows which Nature provides with
such endless variety for her children, and
to which we are admitted on the bare condition of having eyes, should be so generally
neglected. To be sure, eyes are not so common as people think, or poets would be
plentier, and perhaps also these exhibitions
of hers are cheapened in estimation by the
fact that in enjoying them we are not getting the better of anybody else. Your true
lovers of nature, however, contrive to get even
this solace ; and Wordsworth looking upon
mountains as his own peculiar sweethearts,
was jealous of anybody else who ventured
upon even the most innocent flirtation with
them. As if *such* fellows, indeed, could pre-
tend to that nicer sense of what-d'ye-call-it
which was so remarkable in him ! Marry

come up ! Mountains, no doubt, may in-
spire a profounder and more exclusive passion,
but on the whole I am not sorry to have
been born and bred among more domestic
scenes, where I can be hospitable without a
pang.   I am going to ask you presently to
take potluck with me at a board where Winter shall supply whatever there is of cheer.

I think the old fellow has hitherto had
scant justice done him in the main.   We
make him the symbol of old age or death,
and think we have settled the matter.   As if
old age were never kindly as well as frosty ;
as if it had no reverend graces of its own as
good in their way as the noisy impertinence of
childhood, the elbowing self-conceit of youth,
or the pompous mediocrity of middle life !
As if there were anything discreditable in
death, or nobody had ever longed for it!   Suppose we grant that Winter is the sleep of the
year, what then ?   I take it upon me to say
that his dreams are finer than the best reality
of his waking rivals.

"Sleep, Silence' child, the father of soft Rest,"

is a very agreeable acquaintance, and most
of us are better employed in his company
than anywhere else. For my own part, I
think Winter a pretty wide-awake old boy,
and his bluff sincerity and hearty· ways are
more congenial to my mood, and more wholesome for me, than any charms of which his
rivals are capable. Spring is a fickle mis-
tress, who either does not know her own
mind, or is so long in making it up, whether
you shall have her or not have her, that
one gets tired at last of her pretty miffs and
reconciliations. You go to her to be cheered
up a bit, and ten to one catch her in the
sulks, expecting you to find enough good-
humor for both. After she has become
Mrs. Summer she grows a little more staid
in her demeanor ; and her abundant table,
where you are sure to get the earliest fruits
and vegetables of the season, is a good foun-
dation for steady friendship ; but she has
lost that delicious aroma of maidenhood, and
what was delicately rounded grace in the
girl gives more than hints of something like
redundance in the matron. Autumn is the

poet of the family. He gets you up a splendor that you would say was made out of real sunset; but it is nothing more than a few hectic leaves, when all is done. He is but a sentimentalist, after all; a kind of Lamartine whining along the ancestral avenues he has made bare timber of, and begging a contribution of good-spirits from your own savings to keep him in countenance. But Winter has his delicate sensibilities too, only he does not make them as good as indelicate by thrusting them forever in your face. He is a better poet than Autumn, when he has a mind, but, like a truly great one as he is, he brings you down to your bare manhood, and bids you understand him out of that, with no adventitious helps of association, or he will none of you. He does not touch those melancholy chords on which Autumn is as great a master as Heine. Well, is there no such thing as thrumming on them and maundering over them till they get out of tune, and you wish some manly hand would crash through them and leave them dangling brokenly forever? Take Winter as you find

him, and he turns out to be a thoroughly
honest fellow, with no nonsense in him, and
tolerating none in you, which is a great com-
fort in the long run.   He is not what they
call a genial critic ; but bring a real man
along with you, and you will find there is a
crabbed generosity about the old cynic that
you would not exchange for all the creamy
concessions of Autumn.   " Season of mists
and mellow fruitfulness," quotha ?   That 's
just it ; Winter soon blows your head clear
of fog and makes you see things as they are ;
I thank him for it !   The truth is, between
ourselves, I have a very good opinion of the
whole family, who always welcome me without making me feel as if I were too much of
a poor relation.   There ought to be some
kind of distance, never so little, you know,
to give the true relish.   They are as good
company, the worst of them, as any I know,
and I am not a little flattered by a condescension from any one of them ; but I hap-
pen to hold Winter's retainer, this time, and,
like an honest advocate, am bound to make
as good a showing as I can for him, even if

it cost a few slurs upon the rest of the household. Moreover, Winter is coming, and one would like to get on the blind side of him.

The love of Nature in and for herself, or as a mirror for the moods of the mind, is a modern thing. The fleeing to her as an escape from man was brought into fashion by Rousseau ; for his prototype Petrarch, though he had a taste for pretty scenery, had a true antique horror for the grander aspects of nature. He got once to the top of Mont Ventoux, but it is very plain that he did not enjoy it. Indeed, it is only within a century or so that the search after the picturesque has been a safe employment. It is not so even now in Greece or Southern Italy. Where the Anglo-Saxon carves his cold fowl, and leaves the relics of his picnic, the ancient or mediæval man might be pretty confident that some ruffian would try the edge of his knife on a chicken of the Platonic sort, and leave more precious bones as an offering to the genius of the place. The ancients were certainly more social than we, though that, perhaps, was natural enough, when a good part of the world was still covered with forest. They huddled together in cities as well for safety as to keep their minds warm. The Romans had a fondness for country life, but they had fine roads, and Rome was always within easy reach. The author of the Book of Job is the earliest I know of who showed any profound sense of the moral meaning of the outward world ; and I think none has approached him since, though Wordsworth comes nearest with the first two books of the " Prelude." But their feeling is not precisely of the kind I speak of as modern, and which gave rise to what is called descriptive poetry. Chaucer opens his Clerk's Tale with a bit of landscape admirable for its large style, and as well composed as any Claude.

" There is right at the west end of Itaille,
  Down at the root of Vesulus the cold,
  A lusty plain abundant of vitaille,
  Where many a tower and town thou mayst behold,
    hold,
  That founded were in time of fathers old,
  And many an other délectable sight ;
  And Salucës this noble country hight."

What an airy precision of touch there is here, and what a sure eye for the points of character in landscape ! But the picture is altogether subsidiary. No doubt the works of Salvator Rosa and Gaspar Poussin show that there must have been some amateur taste for the grand and terrible in scenery ; but the British poet Thomson ("sweet-souled " is Wordsworth's apt word) was the first to do with words what they had done partially with colors. He was turgid, no good me-trist, and his English is like a translation from one of those poets who wrote in Latin after it was dead ; but he was a man of sin-cere genius, and not only English, but Euro-pean literature is largely in his debt. He was the inventor of cheap amusement for the million, to be had of All-out-doors for the asking. It was his impulse which uncon-sciously gave direction to Rousseau, and it is to the school of Jean Jacques that we owe St. Pierre, Cowper, Châteaubriand, Words-worth, Byron, Lamartine, George Sand, Rus-kin, — the great painters of ideal landscape.

So long as men had slender means, wheth-

er of keeping out cold or checkmating it
with artificial heat, Winter was an unwel-
come guest, especially in the country. There
he was the bearer of a *lettre de cachet*, which
shut its victims in solitary confinement with
few resources but to boose round the fire and
repeat ghost-stories, which had lost all their
freshness and none of their terror. To go to
bed was to lie awake of cold, with an added
shudder of fright whenever a loose casement
or a waving curtain chose to give you the
goose-flesh. Bussy Rabutin, in one of his
letters, gives us a notion how uncomfortable it was in the country, with green wood,
smoky chimneys, and doors and windows that
thought it was their duty to make the wind
whistle, not to keep it out. With fuel so
dear, it could not have been much better
in the city, to judge by Ménage's warning
against the danger of our dressing-gowns tak-
ing fire, while we cuddle too closely over the
sparing blaze. The poet of Winter himself
is said to have written in bed, with his hand
through a hole in the blanket ; and we may
suspect that it was the warmth quite as

much as the company that first drew men together at the coffee-house. Coleridge, in January, 1800, writes to Wedgewood : " I am sitting by a fire in a rug great-coat. . . . . It is most barbarously cold, and you, I fear, can shield yourself from it only by perpetual imprisonment." This thermometrical view of winter is, I grant, a depressing one ; for I think there is nothing so demoralizing as cold. I know of a boy who, when his father, a bitter economist, was brought home dead, said only, " Now we can burn as much wood as we like." I would not off-hand prophesy the gallows for that boy. I remember with a shudder a pinch I got from the cold once in a railroad-car. A born fanatic of fresh air, I found myself glad to see the windows hermetically sealed by the freezing vapor of our breath, and plotted the assassination of the conductor every time he opened the door. I felt myself sensibly barbarizing, and would have shared Colonel Jack's bed in the ash-hole of the glass-furnace with a grateful heart. Since then I have had more charity for the prevailing ill-opinion of win-

ter. It was natural enough that Ovid should
measure the years of his exile in Pontus by
the number of winters.

> Ut sumus in Ponto, ter frigore constitit Ister,
>   Facta est Euxini dura ter unda maris:

> Thrice hath the cold bound Ister fast, since I
> In Pontus was, thrice Euxine's wave made hard.

Jubinal has printed an Anglo-Norman piece
of doggerel in which Winter and Summer
dispute which is the better man. It is not
without a kind of rough and inchoate humor,
and I like it because old Whitebeard gets
tolerably fair play. The jolly old fellow
boasts of his rate of living, with that contempt of poverty which is the weak spot in
the burly English nature.

> Jà Dieu ne place que me avyenge
> Que ne face plus honour
> Et plus despenz en un soul jour
> Que vus en tote vostre vie:

> Now God forbid it hap to me
> That I make not more great display,
> And spend more in a single day
> Than you can do in all your life.

The best touch, perhaps, is Winter's claim for credit as a mender of the highways, which was not without point when every road in Europe was a quagmire during a good part of the year unless it was bottomed on some remains of Roman engineering.

> Je su, fet-il, seignur et mestre
> Et à bon droit le dey estre,
> Quant le la bowe facé saucé
> Par un petit de geglé.

> Master and lord I am, says he,
> And of good right so ought to be,
> Since I make causeys, safely crost,
> Of mud, with just a pinch of frost.

But there is no recognition of Winter as the best of outdoor company.

Even Emerson, an open-air man, and a bringer of it, if ever any, confesses,

> " The frost-king ties my fumbling feet,
>   Sings in my ear, my hands are stones,
>   Curdles the blood to the marble bones,
>   Tugs at the heartstrings, numbs the sense,
>   And hems in life with narrowing fence."

Winter was literally "the inverted year,"
as Thomson called him ; for such entertain-
ments as could be had must be got within
doors.   What cheerfulness there was in bru-
mal verse was that of Horace's *dissolve frigus
ligna super foco large reponens,* so pleasantly
associated with the cleverest scene in Roder-
ick Random.   This is the tone of that poem
of Walton's friend Cotton, which won the
praise of Wordsworth : —

> "Let us home,
> Our mortal enemy is come ;
> Winter and all his blustering train
> Have made a voyage o'er the main.
>   .   .   .   .   .
>
> " Fly, fly, the foe advances fast ;
> Into our fortress let us haste,
> Where all the roarers of the north
> Can neither storm nor starve us forth.
>
> " There underground a magazine
> Of sovereign juice is cellared in,
> Liquor that will the siege maintain
> Should Phœbus ne'er return again.
>   .   .   .   .   .
>
> " Whilst we together jovial sit
> Careless, and crowned with mirth and wit,

> Where, though bleak winds confine us home,
> Our fancies round the world shall roam."

Thomson's view of Winter is also, on the whole, a hostile one, though he does justice to his grandeur.

> "Thus Winter falls,
> A heavy gloom oppressive o'er the world,
> Through Nature shedding influence malign."

He finds his consolations, like Cotton, in the house, though more refined : —

> "While without
> The ceaseless winds blow ice, be my retreat
> Between the groaning forest and the shore
> Beat by the boundless multitude of waves,
> A rural, sheltered, solitary scene,
> Where ruddy fire and beaming tapers join
> To cheer the gloom.   There studious let me sit
> And hold high converse with the mighty dead."

Doctor Akenside, a man to be spoken of with respect, follows Thomson. With him, too, "Winter desolates the year," and

> "How pleasing wears the wintry night
> Spent with the old illustrious dead !
> While by the taper's trembling light

> I seem those awful scenes to tread
> Where chiefs or legislators lie," &c.

Akenside had evidently been reading
Thomson.   He had the conceptions of a
great poet with less faculty than many a
little one, and is one of those versifiers of
whom it is enough to say that we are always
willing to break him off in the middle with
an &c., well knowing that what follows is
but the coming-round again of what went
before, marching in a circle with the cheap
numerosity of a stage-army.   In truth, it
is no wonder that the short days of that
cloudy northern climate should have added
to winter a gloom borrowed of the mind.
We hardly know, till we have experienced
the contrast, how sensibly our winter is alle-
viated by the longer daylight and the pel-
lucid atmosphere.   I once spent a winter in
Dresden, a southern climate compared with
England, and really almost lost my respect
for the sun when I saw him groping among
the chimney-pots opposite my windows as
he described his impoverished arc in the
sky.   The enforced seclusion of the season

makes it the time for serious study and oc-
cupations that demand fixed incomes of un-
broken time.   This is why Milton said "that
his vein never happily flowed but from the
autumnal equinox to the vernal," though in
his twentieth year he had written, on the return of spring, —

> Fallor? an et nobis redeunt in carmina vires
> Ingeniumque mihi munere veris adest?

> Err I? or do the powers of song return
> To me, and genius too, the gifts of Spring?

Goethe, so far as I remember, was the first
to notice the cheerfulness of snow in sunshine.   His *Harz-reise im Winter* gives no
hint of it, for that is a diluted reminiscence
of Greek tragic choruses and the Book of
Job in nearly equal parts.   In one of the
singularly interesting and characteristic letters to Frau von Stein, however, written
during the journey, he says : " It is beautiful indeed ; the mist heaps itself together in
light snow-clouds, the sun looks through,
and the snow over everything gives back a

feeling of gayety." But I find in Cowper
the first recognition of a general amiability
in Winter. The gentleness of his temper,
and the wide charity of his sympathies, made
it natural for him to find good in everything
except the human heart. A dreadful creed
distilled from the darkest moments of dys-
peptic solitaries compelled him against his
will to see in *that* the one evil thing made
by a God whose goodness is over all his
works. Cowper's two walks in the morning and noon of a winter's day are delightful, so long as he contrives to let himself be
happy in the graciousness of the landscape.
Your muscles grow springy, and your lungs
dilate with the crisp air as you walk along
with him. You laugh with him at the gro-
tesque shadow of your legs lengthened across
the snow by the just-risen sun. I know
nothing that gives a purer feeling of outdoor exhilaration than the easy verses of this
escaped hypochondriac. But Cowper also
preferred his sheltered garden-walk to those
robuster joys, and bitterly acknowledged the
depressing influence of the darkened year.

In December, 1780, he writes : "At this season of the year, and in this gloomy uncomfortable climate, it is no easy matter for the owner of a mind like mine to divert it from sad subjects, and to fix it upon such as may administer to its amusement." Or was it because he was writing to the dreadful Newton ? Perhaps his poetry bears truer witness to his habitual feeling, for it is only there that poets disenthral themselves of their reserve and become fully possessed of their greatest charm, — the power of being franker than other men. In the Third Book of the Task he boldly affirms his preference of the country to the city even in winter : —

"But are not wholesome airs, though unperfumed
  By roses, and clear suns, though scarcely felt,
  And groves, if inharmonious, yet secure
  From clamor, and whose very silence charms,
  To be preferred to smoke ? . . . .
  They would be, were not madness in the head
  And folly in the heart ; were England now
  What England was, plain, hospitable kind,
  And undebauched."

The conclusion shows, however, that he was thinking mainly of fireside delights, not

of the blusterous companionship of nature.
This appears even more clearly in the
Fourth Book : —

"O Winter, ruler of the inverted year";

but I cannot help interrupting him to say
how pleasant it always is to track poets
through the gardens of their predecessors
and find out their likings by a flower
snapped off here and there to garnish their
own nosegays. Cowper had been reading
Thomson, and "the inverted year" pleased
his fancy with its suggestion of that starry
wheel of the zodiac moving round through
its spaces infinite. He could not help lov-
ing a handy Latinism (especially with elision
beauty added), any more than Gray, any
more than Wordsworth, — on the sly. But
the member for Olney has the floor : —

"O Winter, ruler of the inverted year,
  Thy scattered hair with sleet like ashes filled,
  Thy breath congealed upon thy lips, thy cheeks
  Fringed with a beard made white with other snows
  Than those of age, thy forehead wrapt in clouds,
  A leafless branch thy sceptre, and thy throne
  A sliding car, indebted to no wheels,

But urged by storms along its slippery way,
I love thee all unlovely as thou seem'st,
And dreaded as thou art !   Thou hold'st the sun
A prisoner in the yet undawning east,
Shortening his journey between morn and noon,
And hurrying him, impatient of his stay,
Down to the rosy west, but kindly still
Compensating his loss with added hours
Of social converse and instructive ease,
And gathering at short notice, in one group,
The family dispersed, and fixing thought,
Not less dispersed by daylight and its cares.
I crown thee king of intimate delights,
Fireside enjoyments, homeborn happiness,
And all the comforts that the lowly roof
Of undisturbed Retirement, and the hours
Of long uninterrupted evening know."

I call this a good *human* bit of writing,
imaginative, too, — not so flushed, not so
. . . . highfaluting (let me dare the odious
word !) as the modern style since poets have
got hold of a theory that imagination is
common-sense turned inside out, and not
common-sense sublimed, — but wholesome,
masculine, and strong in the simplicity of a
mind wholly occupied with its theme.   To

me Cowper is still the best of our descriptive poets for every-day wear. And what unobtrusive skill he has ! How he heightens, for example, your sense of winter-evening seclusion, by the twanging horn of the postman on the bridge ! That horn has rung in my ears ever since I first heard it, during the consulate of the second Adams. Wordsworth strikes a deeper note ; but does it not sometimes come over one (just the least in the world) that one would give anything for a bit of nature pure and simple, without quite so strong a flavor of W. W. ? W. W. is, of course, sublime and all that — but ! For my part, I will make a clean breast of it, and confess that I can't look at a mountain without fancying the late laureate's gigantic Roman nose thrust between me and it, and thinking of Dean Swift's profane version of *Romanos rerum dominos* into *Roman nose ! a rare un ! dom your nose !* But do I judge verses, then, by the impression made on me by the man who wrote them ? Not so fast, my good friend, but, for good or evil, the character and its intellectual product are inextricably interfused.

If I remember aright, Wordsworth himself (except in his magnificent skating-scene
in the "Prelude") has not much to say for
winter out of doors. I cannot recall any
picture by him of a snow-storm. The
reason may possibly be that in the Lake
Country even the winter storms bring rain
rather than snow. He was thankful for the
Christmas visits of Crabb Robinson, because
they "helped him through the winter."
His only hearty praise of winter is when, as
Général Février, he defeats the French : —

"Humanity, delighting to behold
　A fond reflection of her own decay,
　Hath painted Winter like a traveller old,
　Propped on a staff, and, through the sullen day,
　In hooded mantle, limping o'er the plain
　As though his weakness were disturbed by pain :
　Or, if a juster fancy should allow
　An undisputed symbol of command,
　The chosen sceptre is a withered bough
　Infirmly grasped within a withered hand.
　These emblems suit the helpless and forlorn ;
　But mighty Winter the device shall scorn."

　The Scottish poet Grahame, in his "Sab-
bath," says manfully : —

> "Now is the time
> To visit Nature in her grand attire";

and he has one little picture which no other
poet has surpassed : —

> "High-ridged the whirlëd drift has almost reached
> The powdered keystone of the churchyard porch :
> Mute hangs the hooded bell; the tombs lie buried."

Even in our own climate, where the sun
shows his winter face as long and as brightly
as in Central Italy, the seduction of the
chimney-corner is apt to predominate in the
mind over the severer satisfactions of muffled fields and penitential woods. The very
title of Whittier's delightful "Snow-Bound"
shows what *he* was thinking of, though he
does vapor a little about digging out paths.
The verses of Emerson, perfect as a Greek
fragment (despite the archaism of a dissyl-
labic fire), which he has chosen for his epi-
graph, tell us, too, how the

> "Housemates sit
> Around the radiant fireplace, enclosed
> In a tumultuous privacy of storm."

They are all in a tale. It is always the *tristis Hiems* of Virgil. Catch one of them having a kind word for old Barbe Fleurie, unless he whines through some cranny, like a beggar, to heighten their enjoyment while they toast their slippered toes. I grant there is a keen relish of contrast about the bickering flame as it gives an emphasis beyond Gherardo della Notte to loved faces, or kindles the gloomy gold of volumes scarce less friendly, especially when a tempest is blundering round the house. Wordsworth has a fine touch that brings home to us the comfortable contrast of without and within, during a storm at night, and the passage is highly characteristic of a poet whose inspiration always has an undertone of *bourgeois*: —

"How touching, when, at midnight, sweep
    Snow-muffled winds, and all is dark,
 To hear, — and sink again to sleep !"

J. H., one of those choice poets who will not tarnish their bright fancies by publication, always insists on a snow-storm as essen-

tial to the true atmosphere of whist. Mrs.
Battles, in her famous rule for the game, im-
plies winter, and would doubtless have added
tempest, if it could be had for the asking. For
a good solid read also, into the small hours,
there is nothing like that sense of safety
against having your evening laid waste,
which Euroclydon brings, as he bellows
down the chimney, making your fire gasp,
or rustles snow-flakes against the pane with
a sound more soothing than silence. Emerson, as he is apt to do, not only hit the nail
on the head, but drove it home, in that last
phrase of the "tumultuous privacy."

But I would exchange this, and give something to boot, for the privilege of walking
out into the vast blur of a north-northeast
snow-storm, and getting a strong draught on
the furnace within, by drawing the first fur-
rows through its sandy drifts. I love those

> "Noontide twilights which snow makes
> With tempest of the blinding flakes."

If the wind veer too much toward the east,
you get the heavy snow that gives a true

Alpine slope to the boughs of your ever-
greens, and traces a skeleton of your elms in
white ; but you must have plenty of north
in your gale if you want those driving nettles
of frost that sting the cheeks to a crimson
manlier than that of fire. During the great
storm of two winters ago, the most robustious
periwig-pated fellow of late years, I waded
and floundered a couple of miles through the
whispering night, and brought home that
feeling of expansion we have after being in
good company. "Great things doeth He
which we cannot comprehend ; for he saith
to the snow, 'Be thou on the earth.'"

There is admirable snow scenery in Judd's
" Margaret," but some one has confiscated
my copy of that admirable book, and, perhaps, Homer's picture of a snow-storm is the
best yet in its large simplicity : —

" And as in winter-time, when Jove his cold sharp
    javelins throws
Amongst us mortals, and is moved to white the
    earth with snows,
The winds asleep, he freely pours till highest
    prominents,

Hill-tops, low meadows, and the fields that crown
  with most contents
The toils of men, seaports and shores, are hid,
  and every place,
But floods, that fair snow's tender flakes, as their
  own brood, embrace."

Chapman, after all, though he makes very free with him, comes nearer Homer than anybody else. There is nothing in the original of that fair snow's tender flakes, but neither Pope nor Cowper could get out of their heads the Psalmist's tender phrase, " He giveth his snow like wool," for which also Homer affords no hint. Pope talks of " dissolving fleeces," and Cowper of a " fleecy mantle." But David is nobly simple, while Pope is simply nonsensical, and Cowper pretty. If they must have prettiness, Martial would have supplied them with it in his

Densum tacitarum vellus aquarum,

which is too pretty, though I fear it would have pleased Dr. Donne. Eustathius of Thessalonica calls snow ὕδωρ ἐρίωδες, woolly water, which a poor old French poet, Godeau, has amplified into this : —

Lorsque la froidure inhumaine
De leur verd ornement depouille les forêts
Sous une neige épaisse il couvre les guérets,
Et la neige a pour eux la chaleur de la laine.

In this, as in Pope's version of the passage in Homer, there is, at least, a sort of suggestion of snow-storm in the blinding drift of words. But, on the whole, if one would know what snow is, I should advise him not to hunt up what the poets have said about it, but to look at the sweet miracle itself.

The preludings of Winter are as beautiful as those of Spring. In a gray December day, when, as the farmers say, it is too cold to snow, his numbed fingers will let fall doubtfully a few star-shaped flakes, the snow-drops and anemones that harbinger his more assured reign. Now, and now only, may be seen, heaped on the horizon's eastern edge, those "blue clouds" from forth which Shakespeare says that Mars "doth pluck the masoned turrets." Sometimes also, when the sun is low, you will see a single cloud trailing a flurry of snow along the southern hills in a wavering fringe of purple.

And when at last the real snow-storm comes,
it leaves the earth with a virginal look on
it that no other of the seasons can rival, —
compared with which, indeed, they seem
soiled and vulgar.

And what is there in nature so beautiful
as the next morning after such confusion of
the elements ? Night has no silence like
this of busy day. All the batteries of noise
are spiked. We see the movement of life as
a deaf man sees it, a mere wraith of the
clamorous existence that inflicts itself on our
ears when the ground is bare. The earth is
clothed in innocence as a garment. Every
wound of the landscape is healed ; whatever
was stiff has been sweetly rounded as the
breasts of Aphrodite ; what was unsightly
has been covered gently with a soft splendor,
as if, Cowley would have said, Nature had
cleverly let fall her handkerchief to hide it.
If the Virgin (*Nôtre Dame de la neige*) were
to come back, here is an earth that would
not bruise her foot nor stain it. It is

" The fanned snow
That 's bolted by the northern blasts twice o'er,"—

Soffiata e stretta dai venti Schiavi,
Winnowed and packed by the Sclavonian winds, —

packed so hard sometimes on hill-slopes that
it will bear your weight. What grace is in
all the curves, as if every one of them had
been swept by that inspired thumb of Phid-
ias's journeyman !

Poets have fancied the footprints of the
wind in those light ripples that sometimes
scurry across smooth water with a sudden
blur. But on this gleaming hush the aerial
deluge has left plain marks of its course ;
and in gullies through which it rushed tor-
rent-like, the eye finds its bed irregularly
scooped like that of a brook in hard beach-
sand, or, in more sheltered spots, traced with
outlines like those left by the sliding edges
of the surf upon the shore. The air, after
all, is only an infinitely thinner kind of
water, such as I suppose we shall have to
drink when the state does her whole duty as
a moral reformer. Nor is the wind the only
thing whose trail you will notice on this
sensitive surface. You will find that you

have more neighbors and night visitors than you dreamed of. Here is the dainty foot-print of a cat ; here a dog has looked in on you like an amateur watchman to see if all is right, slumping clumsily about in the mealy treachery. And look ! before you were up in the morning, though you were a punctual courtier at the sun's levee, here has been a squirrel zigzagging to and fro like a hound gathering the scent, and some tiny bird searching for unimaginable food, — perhaps for the tinier creature, whatever it is, that drew this slender continuous trail like those made on the wet beach by light borderers of the sea. The earliest autographs were as frail as these. Poseidon traced his lines, or giant birds made their mark, on preadamite sea-margins ; and the thunder-gust left the tear-stains of its sudden passion there ; nay, we have the signatures of delicatest fern-leaves on the soft ooze of æons that dozed away their dreamless leisure before conscious-ness came upon the earth with man. Some whim of nature locked them fast in stone for us after-thoughts of creation. Which of

us shall leave a footprint as imperishable as
that of the ornithorhyncus, or much more
so than that of these Bedouins of the snow-
desert? Perhaps it was only because the
ripple and the rain-drop and the bird were
not thinking of themselves, that they had
such luck. The chances of immortality de-
pend very much on that. How often have
we not seen poor mortals, dupes of a season's
notoriety, carving their names on seeming-
solid rock of merest beach-sand, whose feeble
hold on memory shall be washed away by
the next wave of fickle opinion! Well, well,
honest Jacques, there are better things to be
found in the snow than sermons.

The snow that falls damp comes commonly
in larger flakes from windless skies, and is
the prettiest of all to watch from under cover.
This is the kind Homer had in mind; and
Dante, who had never read him, compares
the *dilatate falde*, the flaring flakes, of his
fiery rain, to those of snow among the mountains without wind. This sort of snowfall
has no fight in it, and does not challenge you
to a wrestle like that which drives well from

the northward, with all moisture thoroughly
winnowed out of it by the frosty wind.
Burns, who was more out of doors than most
poets, and whose barefoot Muse got the color
in her cheeks by vigorous exercise in all
weathers, was thinking of this drier deluge,
when he speaks of the " whirling drift," and
tells how

> " Chanticleer
> Shook off the powthery snaw."

But the damper and more deliberate falls
have a choice knack at draping the trees ;
and about eaves or stone-walls, wherever,
indeed, the evaporation is rapid, and it finds
a chance to cling, it will build itself out in
curves of wonderful beauty. I have seen
one of these dumb waves, thus caught in the
act of breaking, curl four feet beyond the
edge of my roof and hang there for days, as
if Nature were too well pleased with her
work to let it crumble from its exquisite
pause. After such a storm, if you are lucky
enough to have even a sluggish ditch for
a neighbor, be sure to pay it a visit. You
will find its banks corniced with what seems

precipitated light, and the dark current down below gleams as if with an inward lustre. Dull of motion as it is, you never saw water that seemed alive before. It has a brightness, like that of the eyes of some smaller animals, which gives assurance of life, but of a life foreign and unintelligible.

A damp snow-storm often turns to rain, and, in our freakish climate, the wind will whisk sometimes into the northwest so suddenly as to plate all the trees with crystal before it has swept the sky clear of its last cobweb of cloud. Ambrose Philips, in a poetical epistle from Copenhagen to the Earl of Dorset, describes this strange confectionery of Nature, — for such, I am half ashamed to say, it always seems to me, recalling the "glorified sugar-candy" of Lamb's first night at the theatre. It has an artificial air, altogether beneath the grand artist of the atmosphere, and besides does too much mischief to the trees for a philodendrist to take unmixed pleasure in it. Perhaps it deserves a poet like Philips, who really loved Nature and yet liked her to be mighty fine, as Pepys

would say, with a heightening of powder and
rouge : —

" And yet but lately have I seen e'en here
The winter in a lovely dress appear.
Ere yet the clouds let fall the treasured snow,
Or winds begun through hazy skies to blow,
At evening a keen eastern breeze arose,
And the descending rain unsullied froze.
Soon as the silent shades of night withdrew,
The ruddy noon disclosed at once to view
The face of Nature in a rich disguise,
And brightened every object to my eyes ;
For every shrub, and every blade of grass,
And every pointed thorn, seemed wrought in glass;
In pearls and rubies rich the hawthorns show,
And through the ice the crimson berries glow ;
The thick-sprung reeds, which watery marshes yield,
Seem polished lances in a hostile field ;
The stag in limpid currents with surprise
Sees crystal branches on his forehead rise ;
The spreading oak, the beech, the towering pine,
Glazed over in the freezing ether shine ;
The frighted birds the rattling branches shun,
Which wave and glitter in the distant sun,
When, if a sudden gust of wind arise,
The brittle forest into atoms flies,
The crackling wood beneath the tempest bends
And in a spangled shower the prospect ends."

It is not uninstructive to see how tolerable ⌐
Ambrose is, so long as he sticks manfully
to what he really saw.   The moment he
undertakes to improve on Nature he sinks
into the mere court poet, and we surrender
him to the jealousy of Pope without a sigh.
His "rattling branches" and " crackling forest " are good, as truth always is after a fashion ; but what shall we say of that dreadful
stag which, there is little doubt, he valued
above all the rest, because it was purely his
own ?

The damper snow tempts the amateur
architect and sculptor.   His Pentelicus has
been brought to his very door, and if there
are boys to be had (whose company beats all
other recipes for prolonging life) a middle-
aged Master of the Works will knock the
years off his account and make the family
Bible seem a dealer in foolish fables, by a
few hours given heartily to this business.
First comes the Sisyphean toil of rolling the
clammy balls till they refuse to budge farther.   Then, if you would play the statuary,
they are piled one upon the other to the

proper height; or if your aim be masonry,
whether of house or fort, they must be
squared and beaten solid with the shovel.
The material is capable of very pretty effects,
and your young companions meanwhile are
unconsciously learning lessons in æsthetics.
From the feeling of satisfaction with which
one squats on the damp floor of his extem-
porized dwelling, I have been led to think
that the backwoodsman must get a sweeter
savor of self-reliance from the house his own
hands have built than Bramante or Sanso-
vino could ever give. Perhaps the fort is
the best thing, for it calls out more masculine qualities and adds the cheer of battle
with that dumb artillery which gives pain
enough to test pluck without risk of serious
hurt. Already, as I write, it is twenty-odd
years ago. The balls fly thick and fast.
The uncle defends the waist-high ramparts
against a storm of nephews, his breast plas-
tered with decorations like another Radet-
sky's. How well I recall the indomitable
good-humor under fire of him who fell in
the front at Ball's Bluff, the silent perti-

nacity of the gentle scholar who got his last hurt at Fair Oaks, the ardor in the charge of the gallant gentleman who, with the death-wound in his side, headed his brigade at Cedar Creek! How it all comes back, and they never come! I cannot again be the Vauban of fortresses in the innocent snow, but I shall never see children moulding their clumsy giants in it without longing to help. It was a pretty fancy of the young Vermont sculptor to make his first essay in this eva-nescent material. Was it a figure of Youth, I wonder? Would it not be well if all artists could begin in stuff as perishable, to melt away when the sun of prosperity began to shine, and leave nothing behind but the gain of practised hands? It is pleasant to fancy that Shakespeare served his apprenticeship at this trade, and owed to it that most pathetic of despairing wishes, —

> "O, that I were a mockery-king of snow,
> Standing before the sun of Bolingbroke,
> To melt myself away in water-drops!"

I have spoken of the exquisite curves of snow surfaces. Not less rare are the tints of

which they are capable, — the faint blue of
the hollows, for the shadows in snow are
always blue, and the tender rose of higher
points, as you stand with your back to the
setting sun and look upward across the soft
rondure of a hillside.   I have seen within a
mile of home effects of color as lovely as
any iridescence of the Silberhorn after sundown.   Charles II., who never said a foolish
thing, gave the English climate the highest
praise when he said that it allowed you more
hours out of doors than any other, and I
think our winter may fairly make the same
boast as compared with the rest of the year.
Its still mornings, with the thermometer
near zero, put a premium on walking. There
is more sentiment in turf, perhaps, and it is
more elastic to the foot ; its silence, too, is
wellnigh as congenial with meditation as that
of fallen pine-tassel ; but for exhilaration
there is nothing like a stiff snow-crust that
creaks like a cricket at every step, and com-
municates its own sparkle to the senses.
The air you drink is *frappé*, all its grosser
particles precipitated, and the dregs of your

blood with them.   A purer current mounts
to the brain, courses sparkling through it,
and rinses it thoroughly of all dejected stuff.
There is nothing left to breed an exhalation
of ill-humor or despondency.   They say that
this rarefied atmosphere has lessened the
capacity of our lungs.   Be it so.   Quart-pots
are for muddier liquor than nectar.   To me,
the city in winter is infinitely dreary, — the
sharp street-corners have such a chill in them,
and the snow so soon loses its maidenhood
to become a mere drab, — "doing shameful
things," as Steele says of politicians, "without being ashamed."   I pine for the Quaker
purity of my country landscape.   I am
speaking, of course, of those winters that
are not niggardly of snow, as ours too often
are, giving us a gravelly dust instead.   Nothing can be unsightlier than those piebald
fields where the coarse brown hide of Earth
shows through the holes of her ragged
ermine.   But even when there is abundance
of snow, I find as I grow older that there
are not so many good crusts as there used to
be.   When I first observed this, I rashly set-

it to the account of that general degeneracy
in nature (keeping pace with the same melancholy phenomenon in man) which forces
itself upon the attention and into the philos-
ophy of middle life. But happening once to
be weighed, it occurred to me that an arch
which would bear fifty pounds could hardly
be blamed for giving way under more than
three times the weight. I have sometimes
thought that if theologians would remember
this in their arguments, and consider that the
man may slump through, with no fault of
his own, where the boy would have skimmed
the surface in safety, it would be better for
all parties. However, when you *do* get a
crust that will bear, and know any brooklet
that runs down a hillside, be sure to go and
take a look at him, especially if your crust is
due, as it commonly is, to a cold snap follow-
ing eagerly on a thaw. You will never find
him so cheerful. As he shrank away after
the last thaw, he built for himself the most
exquisite caverns of ice to run through, if
not "measureless to man" like those of
Alph, the sacred river, yet perhaps more

pleasing for their narrowness than those for
their grandeur. What a cunning silversmith
is Frost ! The rarest workmanship of Delhi
or Genoa copies him but clumsily, as if the
fingers of all other artists were thumbs.
Fernwork and lacework and filigree in endless variety, and under it all the water tin-
kles like a distant guitar, or drums like a
tambourine, or gurgles like the Tokay of an
anchorite's dream. Beyond doubt there is a
fairy procession marching along those frail
arcades and translucent corridors.

> " Their oaten pipes blow wondrous shrill,
>   The hemlock small blow clear."

And hark ! is that the ringing of Titania's
bridle, or the bells of the wee, wee hawk
that sits on Oberon's wrist ? This wonder
of Frost's handiwork may be had every winter, but he can do better than this, though
I have seen it but once in my life. There
had been a thaw without wind or rain, making the air fat with gray vapor. Towards
sundown came that chill, the avant-courier
of a northwesterly gale. Then, though there

was no perceptible current in the atmosphere, the fog began to attach itself in frosty roots and filaments to the southern side of every twig and grass-stem. The very posts had poems traced upon them by this dumb minstrel. Wherever the moist seeds found lodgment grew an inch-deep moss fine as cobweb, a slender coral-reef, argentine, delicate, as of some silent sea in the moon, such as Agassiz dredges when he dreams. The frost, too, can wield a delicate graver, and in fancy leaves Piranesi far behind. He covers your window-pane with Alpine etchings, as if in memory of that sanctuary where he finds shelter even in midsummer.

Now look down from your hillside across the valley. The trees are leafless, but this is the season to study their anatomy, and did you ever notice before how much color there is in the twigs of many of them? And the smoke from those chimneys is so blue it seems like a feeder of the sky into which it flows. Winter refines it and gives it agreeable associations. In summer it suggests cookery or the drudgery of steam-engines,

but now your fancy (if it can forget for
a moment the dreary usurpation of stoves)
traces it down to the fireside and the brightened faces of children.   Thoreau is the only
poet who has fitly sung it.   The wood-cutter
rises before day and

> " First in the dusky dawn he sends abroad
>   His early scout, his emissary, smoke,
>   The earliest, latest pilgrim from his roof,
>   To feel the frosty air ; . . . .
>   And, while he crouches still beside the hearth,
>   Nor musters courage to unbar the door,
>   It has gone down the glen with the light wind
>   And o'er the plain unfurled its venturous wreath,
>   Draped the tree-tops, loitered upon the hill,
>   And warmed the pinions of the early bird ;
>   And now, perchance, high in the crispy air,
>   Has caught sight of the day o'er the earth's edge,
>   And greets its master's eye at his low door
>   As some refulgent cloud in the upper sky."

Here is very bad verse and very good
imagination.   He had been reading Wordsworth, or he would not have made *tree-tops*
an iambus.   In the *Moretum* of Virgil (or,
if not his, better than most of his) is a pretty
picture of a peasant kindling his winter-
morning fire.   He rises before dawn,

Sollicitaque manu tenebras explorat inertes
Vestigatque focum læsus quem denique sensit.
Parvulus exusto remanebat stipite fumus,
Et cinis obductæ celabat lumina prunæ.
Admovet his pronam submissa fronte lucernam,
Et producit acu stupas humore carentes,
Excitat et crebris languentem flatibus ignem ;
Tandem concepto tenebræ fulgore recedunt,
Oppositaque manu lumen defendit ab aura.

With cautious hand he gropes the sluggish dark,
Tracking the hearth which, scorched, he feels erelong.
In burnt-out logs a slender smoke remained,
And raked-up ashes hid the cinders' eyes ;
Stooping, to these the lamp outstretched he nears,
And, with a needle loosening the dry wick,
With frequent breath excites the languid flame.
Before the gathering glow the shades recede,
And his bent hand the new-caught light defends.

Ovid heightens the picture by a single touch : —

Ipse genu poito flammas exsuscitat aura.

Kneeling, his breath calls back to life the flames.

If you walk down now into the woods, you may find a robin or a bluebird among the red-cedars, or a nuthatch scaling deviously the trunk of some hardwood tree with an eye as keen as that of a French soldier foraging for the *pot-au-feu* of his mess. Perhaps a blue-jay shrills *cah cah* in his corvine trebles, or a chickadee

> "Shows feats of his gymnastic play,
>   Head downward, clinging to the spray."

But both him and the snow-bird I love better to see, tiny fluffs of feathered life, as they scurry about in a driving mist of snow, than in this serene air.

Coleridge has put into verse one of the most beautiful phenomena of a winter walk : —

> "The woodman winding westward up the glen
>   At wintry dawn, where o'er the sheep-track's maze
>   The viewless snow-mist weaves a glistening haze,
>   Sees full before him, gliding without tread,
>   An image with a halo round its head."

But this aureole is not peculiar to winter. I have noticed it often in a summer morning, when the grass was heavy with dew, and even later in the day, when the dewless grass was still fresh enough to have a gleam of its own.

For my own part I prefer a winter walk that take in the nightfall and the intense silence that erelong follows it. The evening lamps look yellower by contrast with the snow, and give the windows that hearty look of which our secretive fires have almost robbed them. The stars seem

"To hang, like twinkling winter lamps,
  Among the branches of the leafless trees,"

or, if you are on a hill-top (whence it is sweet to watch the home-lights gleam out one by one), they look nearer than in summer, and appear to take a conscious part in the cold. Especially in one of those stand-stills of the air that forebode a change of weather, the sky is dusted with motes of fire of which the summer-watcher never dreamed. Winter, too, is, on the whole, the triumphant season of the moon, a moon devoid of sentiment, if you choose, but with the refreshment of a purer intellectual light, — the cooler orb of middle life. Who ever saw anything to match that gleam, rather divined than seen, which runs before her over the snow, a breath of light, as she rises on the infinite silence of winter night? High in the heavens, also she seems to bring out some intenser property of cold with her chilly polish. The poets have instinctively noted this. When Goody Blake imprecates a curse of perpetual chill upon Harry Gill, she has

"The cold, cold moon above her head";

and Coleridge speaks of

"The silent icicles,
Quietly gleaming to the quiet moon."

As you walk homeward, — for it is time that we should end our ramble, — you may perchance hear the most impressive sound in nature, unless it be the fall of a tree in the forest during the hush of summer noon. It is the stifled shriek of the lake yonder as the frost throttles it. Wordsworth has described it (too much, I fear, in the style of Dr. Armstrong) : —

"And, interrupting oft that eager game,
From under Esthwaite's splitting fields of ice,
The pent-up air, struggling to free itself,
Gave out to meadow-grounds and hills a loud
Protracted yelling, like the noise of wolves
Howling in troops along the Bothnic main."

Thoreau (unless the English lakes have a different dialect from ours) calls it admirably well a "whoop." But it is a noise like none other, as if Demogorgon were moaning inarticulately from under the earth. Let us get within doors, lest we hear it again, for there is something bodeful and uncanny in it.

Cambridge : Printed by Welch, Bigelow, & Co.